Tamara the Tooth Fairy was originally published
as a Rainbow Magic special. This version has
been specially adapted for developing readers
in conjunction with a Reading Consultant.

Special thanks to
Rachel Elliot and
Fiona Munro

Reading Consultant: Prue Goodwin, lecturer in literacy and children's books.

ORCHARD BOOKS
338 Euston Road, London NW1 3BH
Orchard Books Australia
Level 17/207 Kent Street, Sydney, NSW 2000

A CIP catalogue record for this book is available from the British Library.

ISBN 978 1 40833 632 8

1 3 5 7 9 10 8 6 4 2

Printed in China

The paper and board used in this paperback are natural recyclable products
made from wood grown in sustainable forests. The manufacturing processes
conform to the environmental regulations of the country of origin.

Orchard Books is an imprint of Hachette Children's Group and published by
the Watts Publishing Group Limited, an Hachette UK company.

www.hachette.co.uk

Tamara
the Tooth Fairy

by Daisy Meadows

ORCHARD

www.rainbowmagic.co.uk

The Fairyland Palace

Rachel's House

Bedroom

Garden

Tippington Town

Contents

Story One

The Moonstone Ring

"My wobbly tooth has finally fallen out!" Kirsty Tate called to her best friend. She had arrived just that morning at Rachel Walker's house, where she was staying for part of the summer holidays.

"That's brilliant! We've never met the Tooth Fairy!" said Rachel, as the girls changed into their pyjamas. "I wonder what she's like?"

Climbing into bed, Kirsty put her tooth safely under the pillow. "The Tooth Fairy is so quiet that she never wakes children up," Kirsty yawned.

The two friends had a very special secret. They had often visited Fairyland. Sometimes naughty Jack Frost and his goblins made terrible mischief.

The girls had often helped the fairies defeat them. Rachel smiled and turned out the light. It had been a long day, and the girls were soon asleep.

When Rachel's alarm clock went off in the morning, she sat up and looked eagerly over to where her best friend was sleeping.

Kirsty opened her eyes and lifted her pillow. "My tooth is still here," she said in a disappointed voice.

"The Tooth Fairy is probably

confused because you're staying here instead of at home," Rachel said, jumping out of bed to comfort her friend. "I expect she'll come tonight."

"Perhaps she left a coin and forgot to take the tooth," said Kirsty, picking up the pillow and shaking it. "Or maybe the coin got stuck inside somehow?"

As Kirsty shook the pillow, the girls heard a faint tinkling sound. Then, with a sparkling whoosh, a tiny fairy came shooting out of the pillowcase.

"Hello, Kirsty and Rachel," she said. "I'm Tamara the Tooth Fairy."

"Hello, Tamara," said Rachel.

"Are you here to take Kirsty's tooth?"

"I wish I was," said Tamara sadly. " But I've come to ask for your help."

She waved her wand towards the mirror hanging on the wall, and the surface rippled. When it was smooth again, the girls saw Jack Frost's face scowling out at them!

Jack Frost was sitting on his throne, a hand clamped to the side of his face. He had terrible toothache.

"Perhaps you should see a dentist," one of his goblin servants muttered bravely.

"What did you say?" hissed Jack Frost. "I never want to hear the word 'dentist' in this room again!"

"But how will you get rid of your toothache without a den—?" asked another, timidly.

"If I had that Tooth Fairy's magical objects, I bet my teeth would be perfect,"

Jack Frost snarled at his goblin helpers. "So you are going to steal them for me!"

Tamara turned to the girls. "And that's exactly what happened," she said sadly. "Yesterday, the goblins sneaked into my home and took my magical objects."

"What are they?" asked Kirsty, shocked.

Tamara used her wand to draw each object in the air. The first showed a delicate, shining ring.

"The moonstone ring guides me towards children with loose teeth," she began. "Then, the endless coin helps me exchange the teeth for money," continued Tamara. "And lastly, the enchanted pouch contains all the teeth I've ever taken, ground up into a rare and powerful fairy dust."

"We'll help you get them back!" chorused the girls.

After breakfast, Rachel and Kirsty headed into town. As they walked, they noticed three boys just ahead of them. Something sparkled on the tallest boy's finger.

Tamara was hiding inside Kirsty's shirt pocket, but suddenly she popped her head out.

"Girls," she grinned. "That's the moonstone ring!"

"Those boys are goblins!"

exclaimed Kirsty. "Let's follow them!"

The boys were arguing, and the ring flashed as the tallest goblin waved his hands around. They stopped outside Tippington Dental Surgery. "There will be lots of teeth here," one of them said. "Jack

Frost needs teeth to grind up so he can make magic dust to stop his toothache!"

"Oh no, they're bound to cause trouble in there," said Kirsty.

The receptionist gasped as the goblins burst through the door, with Rachel and Kirsty right behind them.

CRASH! BANG! CLATTER! The goblins quickly turned the surgery into a disaster area. Cupboards were opened and equipment was scattered on the floor.

Suddenly, the tallest goblin rolled into a tall cabinet, which burst open. A cascade of loose teeth rained down on him.

The goblins quickly began scooping them up.

Tamara zoomed out of Kirsty's pocket. "Stop!" she demanded. "Those teeth don't belong to you. Put them back!"

"No way!" snapped the tallest goblin.

Tamara thought quickly.
"Jack Frost won't want
boring old teeth like that," she
said. "Just give us that ring, and
I will magic you each a set of
teeth that are much more fun!"

The goblins looked at one another.

"I bet Jack Frost would be really pleased with three whole sets of teeth," said one.

"It's a deal!" they all said together.

The goblins dropped the dentist's teeth on the floor, and Tamara fluttered over and took her ring, which instantly shrank to fairy size.

Then she waved her wand and each goblin found a set of wind-up teeth in his hand!

The goblins giggled and squawked as they ran off, delighted with their jumping, chattering teeth.

Tamara tidied up the surgery with a swish of her wand before they followed the goblins out hurriedly.

Popping out of Kirsty's pocket, the little fairy beamed and wiggled her hand around in delight, admiring the ring back on her finger. "I must go back to Fairyland now," she said to Kirsty and Rachel.

"You've both been wonderful! I'm sure that if you keep helping me, I'll soon find the endless coin and the enchanted pouch!"

"Of course we'll help you!" said Kirsty.

As the moonstone ring flashed, Tamara twirled into the air and disappeared in a puff of fairy dust.

Story Two

The Endless Coin

Chapter One

In the middle of the night, a muffled squawking sound woke Rachel up.

"Kirsty!" she called out, switching on the light. "I think there's a goblin in the room, trying to steal your tooth!"

There was another squawk and a crash as the light went out again. The silly goblin had knocked the lamp over in the dark.

As Kirsty picked it up and switched it on once more, they realised that the goblin had vanished.

"Perhaps he climbed out of the window," Rachel said. "Did he get your tooth?"

Kirsty felt under her pillow and smiled.

"No," she said. "It's still here."

Bleary-eyed, the girls climbed back into bed and switched off the light. Neither of them had noticed that the wardrobe door was not quite closed

Next morning, the girls dressed and hurried downstairs for breakfast. Kirsty poured out some cereal, but just as she reached for the milk jug, it

started to glow. The girls knew
at once that something magical
was happening.

A puff of silver fairy dust
sparkled, and then Tamara the
Tooth Fairy flew out and gave
a little twirl.

"I've brought some news
from Fairyland," she said in a
bright voice.

The girls listened as Tamara
continued.

"Jack Frost has sent one
of his goblins to the human
world with the endless coin!"

Tamara shook her head. "He's ordered him to bring back as many teeth as he can find."

"Tamara, there was a goblin in our room last night," Rachel said.

The little fairy gasped. "If he was trying to take your tooth, I bet he's got the endless coin."

Suddenly, the three friends heard a noise from upstairs. It was Rachel's dog, Buttons, barking loudly.

The girls looked at each other.

"That's his warning bark," said Rachel, jumping to her feet. "Come on!"

They raced up the stairs, with Tamara zooming above their heads.

"He's in your bedroom, Rachel!" said Kirsty, racing into the room.

Buttons was standing in front of the wardrobe, and wouldn't stop barking.

"What's the matter, Buttons?" Rachel asked, putting her hand on his soft head.

The girls could see now that the wardrobe was slightly open. Rachel, feeling brave, stepped forward and pulled the door.

"EEEEYOWEEE!"

Chapter Two

A squealing bundle fell out
of the wardrobe, and onto the
floor!

The girls saw that the bundle
had two skinny legs, green
arms and a bony green head.

"It's a goblin!" cried Kirsty.

But he wasn't dressed in normal goblin style. He was wearing at least three skirts, two dresses and a woolly hat.

"He's wearing all the clothes in my wardrobe!" Rachel exclaimed. "Put those back at once!" she shouted.

The goblin scowled at her. "Shan't," he said, sticking out his tongue.

"You can't talk to Rachel like that in her own bedroom," said Tamara.

The goblin sneered at her.

"What are you going to do about it, you silly fairy?" he demanded. "You can't do anything because I've got your magic coin. HA!"

"Put my clothes back at once and give Tamara the endless

coin," said Rachel.

Tamara thought fast. "Give me back the endless coin," she said, "and I will use my magic to give you some brand new teeth for Jack Frost."

The goblin thought for a moment. "Really?" he said.

"I promise," said Tamara.

The goblin grabbed one of Rachel's handbags from inside the wardrobe, then held up the glimmering endless coin and dropped it inside.

"Come and get it, then," he said.

As Tamara darted towards the handbag, the goblin smiled.

"No!" cried Rachel suddenly, working out what was happening.

"It's a trap!" Kirsty shouted at the same moment. "Stop!"

But they were both too late. Tamara flew into the bag,

and the goblin snapped it shut.
Tamara the Tooth Fairy was
a prisoner!

"Let her go right now!" said
Kirsty.

"No chance," said the
goblin. "I'm taking her to the
Ice Castle with me, and Jack
Frost will keep her prisoner
until she agrees to give him
every tooth she can find."
With that, the goblin gave a
squawking laugh and ran past
Kirsty, pushing her out of the
way and onto Rachel's bed.

"Hey, stop!" cried Kirsty furiously.

The goblin didn't reply. He ran down the stairs at top speed, clutching his bag to his chest. He hurried out,

slamming the front door
behind him.

"We must follow him!"
Rachel shouted, dashing out of
the door.

The goblin had grabbed a
scooter from a boy playing on
his driveway, and was zooming
off at top speed.

Chapter Three

"We'll never catch him!" said Kirsty.

WOOF!

WOOF!

They heard a loud barking as Buttons raced past and took a flying leap at the scooter!

The goblin was so wrapped up that when he fell onto the pavement he bounced three times, and then couldn't stand up again!

"Good boy, Buttons!" said Kirsty, stopping to catch her breath.

The handbag lay on the pavement. Rachel ran to open it and Tamara zoomed out.

The coin had returned to fairy size and Tamara was happily holding it.

"Thank you, Buttons!"

Tamara smiled and waved her wand at the silly goblin. Instantly, the layers of extra clothes disappeared, and he was furious.

"Give me that coin!" he shouted. "I stole it fair and square!"

Buttons began to growl, and the terrified goblin gave a yell, and ran off as fast as he could.

"You two must go home," said Tamara. "And I must take the endless coin back to Fairyland, but I'll be back soon.

And we can begin searching
for the enchanted pouch!"

Tamara waved her wand
and disappeared in a flurry
of golden sparkles. "Come on,
boy, let's go home," Rachel said
to Buttons.

The three of them hurried back home, stopping on the way to return the scooter.

"What a great start to the day!" said Kirsty.

"Yes, we've helped Tamara to find her second magical object, and we haven't even had breakfast yet!" said Rachel with a laugh. "I have a feeling that this is going to be a very good day!"

Story Three

The Enchanted Pouch

Chapter One

The girls had been playing badminton in the garden all afternoon.

"Amazing shot!" said Rachel, shielding her eyes from the sun. "I can't even see the shuttlecock!"

"There it is," said Kirsty.

"That's not a shuttlecock!" laughed Rachel. "It's Tamara the Tooth Fairy!"

"Hi, girls!" Tamara said with a bright smile. "I've come to ask you a big favour."

They dropped their racquets and ran to greet her. "It's great to see you," said Kirsty.

"Will you come to the Ice Castle with me?" asked the little fairy. "I have to find my enchanted pouch, but Jack Frost's home is a scary place."

"Of course we'll come," said Rachel at once.

"Let's go down to the bottom of the garden," said Kirsty. "No one will be able to see us there." As soon as they were out of sight of the kitchen window, Tamara raised her wand and a stream of glittering fairy dust whooshed from it, curling around the girls like a golden ribbon.

They felt a warm tingle as the fairy magic started to work. The garden around them

disappeared, and gauzy wings appeared on their backs.

A few minutes later the sparkles faded, and they found themselves flying over a forest of snowy trees. Ahead of them, a castle was glittering with ice.

"Look, there's Jack Frost's home," said Rachel. "We're in his land now!"

Rachel, Kirsty and Tamara fluttered down at the edge of the forest. Their feet crunched into fresh snow. Rachel and Kirsty were shivering. Tamara gave her wand a little flick, and instantly they were each snuggling into a thick furry jacket.

They peered up at the turrets of the Ice Castle, and saw an open window close to the top.

"Up there!" Kirsty pointed.
"That's our way in!"

The three friends rose up
and flew towards the window.
Inside, they could hear a
horrible whining sound.

"We're in Jack Frost's bedroom!" Rachel whispered. Jack Frost was sitting up in bed, making a horrible noise.

Chapter Two

He was surrounded by goblin
guards, who were tying a piece
of string around his tooth. They
were going to pull it out!

"No!" Tamara cried. Before
Rachel or Kirsty could stop her,
she flew bravely over to his bed.

"You need to go to the dentist," she said gently. "That's the only way you'll get rid of the pain."

"A fairy!" squawked the silly goblin guards, shooing her away. "In Jack Frost's bedroom!"

"I'm not going to let a dentist torture me!" Jack Forst screeched.

"A dentist isn't going to hurt you at all," said Tamara. "They are there to make you feel better!"

"I'm scared," he replied at last in a small voice.

"Listen," said Rachel. "I've been going to the dentist all my life, and she's never hurt me."

"Really?" asked Jack Frost.

"We'll take you there!" said Tamara. She waved her wand, and in a shower of sparkles, Jack Frost was transformed into a human.

He had hair in place of icy spikes and a T-shirt and jeans in place of pyjamas. With another flash of glittery magic, Rachel and Kirsty were human size again, and they were all standing outside Tippington Dental Surgery.

They marched Jack Frost into reception.

"Hello," smiled Rachel. "We need an emergency appointment please. Our uncle has terrible toothache!"

Jack Frost was very nervous,

but the dentist looked at him
with a warm smile.

"Let's see if we can take
away your pain," she said.

She guided him into the
chair. "Just lean back and try to
relax. Open wide!"

It was all over very quickly.

The dentist pulled out the bad tooth, and gave Jack Frost some blue liquid to rinse out his mouth. Then she dropped the tooth into his hand.

"The pain's completely gone!" he said.

The dentist handed Jack Frost a little bag.

"There is a toothbrush, some toothpaste and moushwash in there," she said. "I would like you to brush your teeth twice a day and eat fewer sweets."

"Thank you very much,"

said Rachel, realising that Jack
Frost wasn't going to be polite
enough to say it himself.

Chapter Three

They made their way out
into the sunshine. Jack Frost
gazed at his spiky rotten tooth
lovingly.

"Isn't it amazing!" he said.
"I'd much rather have this
tooth than some silly pouch."

Was this their chance to get the enchanted pouch back?

Tamara was waiting for them behind the surgery. "That's a wonderful tooth," she said. "If I had my enchanted pouch back, I could make you an icy display stand for it."

At once, Jack Frost reached into his pocket and handed Tamara a little velvet pouch.

The fairy took a pinch of powder from inside and threw it upwards. The shimmering dust came together in mid-air.

Slowly it formed a tiny version of the Ice Castle, complete with a velvet cushion.

Jack Frost gave a gasp of delight and placed his tooth on top. Then he waved his wand and magicked himself back to his icy home.

"Thank you for everything," said Tamara. "Goodbye!"

She winked at them and vanished in a puff of fairy dust.

That night, Kirsty checked her tooth was still under her pillow before going to sleep.

"Has Tamara been?" asked Rachel in the morning.

Kirsty found two objects where her tooth had been. One was a shiny pound coin. The other was a silver ring, with something shimmering inside the stone.

"I know what that is!" Rachel exclaimed excitedly.

"It's your own tooth, transformed into fairy dust!"

"This adventure has been fun," said Kirsty. "I can't wait to lose my next tooth!"

**If you enjoyed this story,
you may want to read**

Alexandra the Royal Baby Fairy Early Reader

Here's how the story begins...

"Are we nearly there, Mum?"
asked Kirsty, leaning as
far forwards in the car as
her seatbelt would let her.
"We can't wait to get to the
palace!"

Mrs Tate turned her head
a little to smile at Kirsty and
her best friend, Rachel Walker.

They were sitting side by side in the back of the car.

"Not long now, girls. When we reach the top of this hill you'll be able to see Norwood Palace straight ahead. Look, there it is!"

Read
Alexandra the Royal Baby Fairy
Early Reader
to find out
what happens next!

Shannon the Ocean Fairy

Summer the Holiday Fairy

Florence the Friendship Fairy

Belle the Birthday Fairy

Kylie the Carnival Fairy

Flora the Fancy Dress Fairy

Mia the Bridesmaid Fairy

Selena the Sleepover Fairy

Destiny the Pop Star Fairy

Start reading with the
Rainbow Magic fairies